For Megan and Laura, my first Beloveds;
and for Ben, Claire, Lucy and Charlie, who inspire me.

ISBN 13: 978-1-63489-139-4

Library of Congress Catalog Number:
  2018909416

  Printed in the United States of America
First Printing: 2018

22 21 20 19 18   5 4 3 2 1

  Cover and interior design
  by Mayfly Design

WISE Ink
CREATIVE ★ PUBLISHING

807 Broadway St. NE, Ste. 46
Minneapolis, Minnesota 55413
www.wiseinkpub.com

To order, visit www.itascabooks.com
or call 1-800-901-3480.
Reseller discounts available.

BELOVED and the PEPPER TREE

Written by Ann Gonzales   Illustrated by Manu Montoya

Beloved was a little girl who lived in a house on a hill. At the bottom of the hill was an old Pepper Tree. The Pepper Tree was Beloved's very best friend.

The Pepper Tree was quite crooked. Her gnarled
and twisted branches made little tufts of leaves that
often shed. Her trunk was split down the middle,
and it grew low and wide.

Beloved thought her friend was beautiful.
She brought pretty ribbons to tie to the
Pepper Tree's branches.

The Pepper Tree was strong and true.
Sometimes, Beloved built snow people to
keep the Pepper Tree company.

The Pepper Tree's shade was cool and comforting.
Beloved loved to sit under her boughs, reading books
or having picnics.

More than anything, Beloved loved to climb the Pepper Tree's branches and imagine she was on stage. She sang for the birds who sang back with their own gift of song.

She sang for the sun that warmed her brown arms.

She sang for her family, her best friend the Pepper Tree, and all the people of the world.

One day, Mama announced that the family would be moving away from the house on the hill. "But what about my Pepper Tree? Won't she move with us?" Beloved asked.

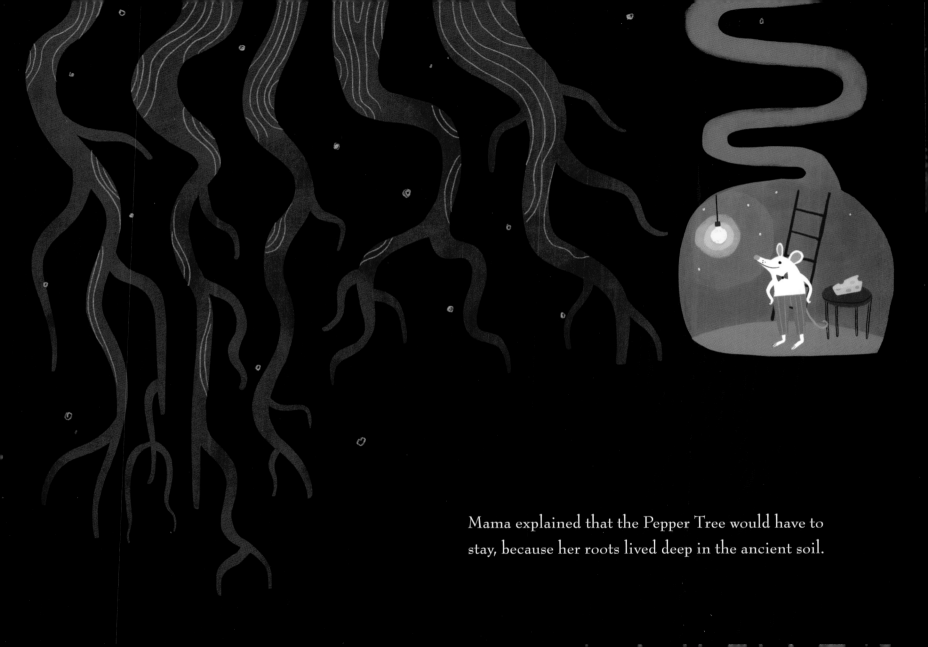

Mama explained that the Pepper Tree would have to stay, because her roots lived deep in the ancient soil.

Beloved began to cry as she ran down the hill to the Pepper Tree.

She threw her arms around her friend's bumpy trunk and breathed in her earthy smell. "Oh, dear Pepper Tree. How could I possibly leave you?"

The Pepper Tree, who had lived a very long time, was as wise as she was loving. "There, there Beloved. All is well. You must leave because it is time for you to grow."

"Grow? But I'm already grown!" Beloved said.

"Beloved, each time we move to a new place, try something new, or make a new friend, we change in ways we could never imagine," the Pepper Tree said.

"But I don't want to change!" Beloved cried.
"I want to stay here with you!"

"If you stay here, Beloved, you will be like a Pepper Tree that grows in a clay pot. You see, a tree can live in a clay pot, but it will stay small. Its roots won't grow deep, its branches won't reach high, and its leaves won't fan out to catch the sun."

Beloved could only cry and hold on tight to her friend.

"Dear Beloved, keep me in your heart, and I will be with you wherever you go."

"I don't know how to do that," Beloved said.

"I will show you in time," said the Pepper Tree. "When it is time to say goodbye, bring a satchel with you."

Beloved did not understand, but she would do as the Pepper Tree asked.

Some days passed, and in those days, all of Beloved's world was packed into boxes. Some boxes were marked "toys," some were marked "clothes," but none were marked "Pepper Tree." One day, a big truck arrived, and two men loaded the boxes inside.

Beloved knew it was time to say goodbye. Tears blurred her sight
as she ran down the hill with her satchel.

"I have a gift for you," the Pepper Tree said.
"What is it?" Beloved asked.
The Pepper Tree smiled, and
hundreds of little seeds fell like
rain around Beloved.

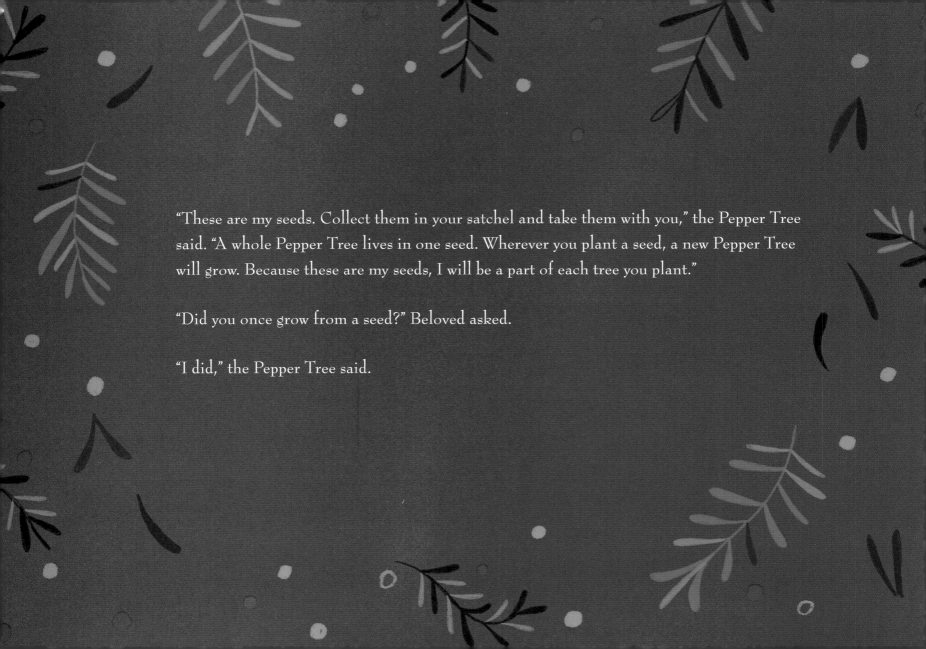

"These are my seeds. Collect them in your satchel and take them with you," the Pepper Tree said. "A whole Pepper Tree lives in one seed. Wherever you plant a seed, a new Pepper Tree will grow. Because these are my seeds, I will be a part of each tree you plant."

"Did you once grow from a seed?" Beloved asked.

"I did," the Pepper Tree said.

Beloved dried her tears. "I will keep your seeds with me wherever I go. When I find a beautiful place, I will plant your seeds in the soil," Beloved said. "Thank you for your gift of friendship, dear Pepper Tree."

Beloved joined her family and left the house on the hill.
Though she was sad, Beloved smiled knowing she carried
her friend in her heart. And in her satchel, new friends
waited to meet her.

Deepest gratitude to Sri Sakthi Amma for The Journey,
Brahman Kyrie for her love and teaching, and all the friends and family who support me.

—ANN GONZALES

. . . .

About the Author

Ann Gonzales is a spiritual seeker, author, and artist who loves to play. She enthusiastically helps children and adults connect with their intuition and passions through expressive arts. When she is not facilitating Art for Healing and Recovery workshops, she can be found in Carlsbad, California cuddling her beloved dog Roxy and Ziggy the cat.

About the Illustrator

Manu Montoya was born in Medellín, Colombia. She studied graphic design and advertising in her home town and art direction in Barcelona where she actually lives. She grew up both in the city and the country, and spent most of her childhood drawing, playing with plants and animals, and exploring the woods. Manu has worked for various advertising agencies and is an illustrator for children's books and other publications.